WALT DISNEY Productions

The Winnie-the-Pooh
Scratch and Sniff Book

Based on a story by
A. A. Milne

Pictures by
the Walt Disney Studio

*In Which Tigger is Unbounced
and Pooh and Piglet Find
Their Way Home by a Nose*

gb Golden Press • New York

Western Publishing Company, Inc.
Racine, Wisconsin

Third Printing, 1975

The Text is published by permission of E. P. Dutton & Co., Inc.,
the publishers of WINNIE-THE-POOH (Copyright, 1926, by E. P. Dutton &
Co., Inc. Copyright Renewal, 1954, by A. A. Milne) and THE HOUSE
AT POOH CORNER (Copyright, 1928, by E. P. Dutton & Co., Inc. Copyright
Renewal, 1956, by A. A. Milne).

Copyright © 1974 Walt Disney Productions. All rights reserved.
Printed in the U.S.A. by Western Publishing Company, Inc.

Library of Congress Catalog Card Number: 74-14158

The ''Microfragrance''™ labels were supplied by 3M Company.

Golden, A Golden Fragrance Book, and Golden Press® are trademarks of
Western Publishing Company, Inc.

One summer morning, Winnie-the-Pooh was sitting quite comfortably in the sunshine. He was just coming to the last line of a new and very nice hum when . . .

POUNCE . . . Pooh rather suddenly found that he was lying flat on his back.

"Hallo, Pooh," said Tigger, who had rather suddenly appeared on Pooh's stomach.

"Hallo, Tigger," said Pooh, but before he had a chance to add on a How-are-you-Tigger or a How-nice-to-see-you-Tigger, Tigger bounced away.

"Tigger's a friendly fellow, all right," said Pooh, getting up and brushing the dust off his stomach, "but he certainly is a Bouncy sort of Tigger."

Meanwhile, in his part of the Forest, Piglet, having just had breakfast, was sweeping up his yard. Suddenly, he too was bounced right off his feet.

"Hallo, Piglet," cried Tigger.

"Oh, Tigger," said Piglet in an uncomfortable sort of voice, the kind of voice a Very Small Animal who had just been bounced by a Very Large Tigger might use.

But before Piglet had a chance to go on, Tigger bounced off into the forest.

KLOVER

A little later, Rabbit was standing happily in his sunny clo-ver patch, enjoying the scent of freshly growing clover.

"Should be ready for eating in a week or so," he was just saying lazily to himself when . . . POUNCE!

And, "Hallo, Rabbit, and goodbye, Rabbit," called Tigger as he bounced past Rabbit and over the last row of clover and then off into the Forest.

"Something has got to be done about Tigger," said Rabbit. "When a rabbit can't relax peacefully in his own clover patch, something has got to be done. And I," he added, "am going to do that very something!"

Scratch and sniff. Here's the smell of fresh clover Rabbit was enjoying so much. Do you like it too?

That afternoon, Rabbit went round and collected Pooh and Piglet for a Very Important Planning Meeting.

"As I was saying," said Rabbit, "as I was saying, POOH! Are you listening?"

Pooh, who had been dreaming lazily of honey, and buzzing bees, and buzzing bee-trees, opened his eyes and blinked. "Whatever you say, Rabbit."

"I didn't say it yet," said Rabbit, "but as I was trying to say — it is time for us to unbounce Tigger."

"How do we do that?" asked Piglet.

"I have made a Plan," announced Rabbit. "Tomorrow, we will take Tigger on a nice long Explore way past the Six Pine Trees and up to the Hundred Acre Wood, and we'll lose him there. We'll lose him so well that he won't be able to bounce himself out. And when we come back for him the next day, he'll be a much humbler Tigger, an Oh-Rabbit-I-*am*-glad-to-see-you-Tigger, and not at all the Bouncy sort of Tigger he is now."

Well, Piglet wasn't quite sure that it would be nice to lose Tigger overnight in the Wood. But Rabbit very kindly explained that, after all, Tigger would be so much nicer to have around after he was unbounced. So when Piglet, who was a Very Small and Easily Bounced Animal, had to admit that an unbounced Tigger would be much nicer, and Pooh, who was still dreaming honey-dreams, made a small contented sound in his honey daydream, Rabbit took it to mean that they were all in agreement with his plan.

Tigger was delighted when the next day Rabbit, Pooh, and Piglet arrived at Kanga's to take him for an Explore. He was so excited, in fact, that he bounced right up from the breakfast table and out the front door.

Pooh, who had eaten just before leaving home, was already wishing he had brought along a Little-Something-Just-in-Case. "What's that you're having for breakfast, Roo?" he said hopefully.

Scratch and sniff to smell Roo's egg custard. Pooh would have liked it, don't you think?

"Hallo, Pooh," squeaked Roo. "I'm having egg custard. Do you like egg custard, Pooh, do you?"

Hush, Roo dear," said Kanga. "Eat your breakfast. You're welcome to join us, Pooh," she added.

"Well, thank you," said Pooh, sliding up to the table. "I was thinking of Something, well, a little bit more honeyish, but perhaps a little smackerel of egg custard would . . ."

"Pooh," said Rabbit sharply, "come on. Tigger's waiting for us."

There was almost a hitch in the plans when Roo decided that he wanted to go with them. Rabbit very quickly explained though that it was really a rather misty and moisty day, not the sort of day for Roos at all, and Kanga said, "No, Roo dear, not today. Some other day perhaps." So it really was just the four of them, Rabbit and Pooh and Piglet and Tigger, going off into the gray woods for their morning's Explore.

The mist got thicker and thicker as they climbed toward the top of the Wood. Every time Tigger bounced on ahead, he disappeared into the gray.

"This is perfect weather," cried Rabbit. "When Tigger bounces off, we'll simply duck into the bushes. He'll never find us in this mist. But we'll wait a few more minutes. We're still too close to home."

"How can you tell, Rabbit?" asked Piglet, peering into the mist for something familiar.

"Easy," answered Rabbit. "I can still smell the Six Pine Trees."

Pooh and Piglet stopped, noses raised, sniffing the misty air.

Scratch and sniff. Are Pooh and Piglet still close to home? Can you smell the Six Pine Trees, too?

Up, up they climbed, right to the top of the Hundred Acre Wood, and as they climbed, Tigger kept bouncing farther and farther away.

Suddenly . . . "NOW!" cried Rabbit. He jumped into a hollow by the side of the path, and Pooh and Piglet followed.

They all crouched together in the underbrush. Everything was very quiet and very gray. They couldn't hear or see anything.

Then, there was a pattering noise on the path, and a big "Halloooo!" Tigger called to them. "Rabbit! Pooh! Piglet! Where are you?" There was a moment of silence. "That's funny," said Tigger, and then they heard him bouncing off.

"Hurrah, we've done it!" cried Rabbit, after a few more minutes of silence.

So Rabbit and Pooh and Piglet set off through the Wood for home. Rabbit was certain that everything was going according to plan, and so it seemed to be, until they began to notice a certain little sandpit. Pooh was sure it was following them, for no matter in which direction they tried to leave it, it always seemed to be lying in wait somewhere around the next corner.

"Rabbit," said Pooh, "I've been thinking. We've been looking for home all this time, and finding this sandpit instead. How would it be this time if we go away from the sandpit, and then try to find our way back to it? Perhaps we will find home instead."

"Really, Pooh," said Rabbit, "you are a Bear of Very Little Brain, and you have just had a very silly idea. If I walk away from this sandpit, and then walk back to it, why of course I should find it."

So Rabbit walked into the mist, and when he had gone a hundred yards, he turned around and started back again towards Pooh and Piglet.

Pooh and Piglet waited and waited. But, after about twenty minutes and no Rabbit, Pooh got up. "Now, Piglet," he said, "let's go home."

"Pooh," squeaked Piglet, all excited, "do you know where home is?"

"No," said Pooh, "but I have twelve pots of honey in my cupboard, and they know where home is because that's where they are and they've been calling to me, only I couldn't hear them properly before, because of Rabbit talking. But now, if we'll quietly listen to our noses, we'll be able to hear and smell them."

"What kind of smell might we be smelling, Pooh?" asked Piglet.

"Well," said Pooh, as his honey-dream look came over his face, "it's a honeyish, it's-time-for-a-smackerel sort of smell, such as might comfort a Bear Lost in the Misty Wood."

"Pooh," cried Piglet, his nose quivering, "I can smell something like that." He trotted off, nose in the air, with Pooh stumping along behind.

Then Piglet stopped by a little bush covered with lovely-to-smell white flowers. "Oh, Pooh," he said. "Here it is already, and it's not your honeypots at all."

"Piglet," said Pooh, "I believe you have found a honey-suckle bush. And it *is* a honeyish sort of smell, and a comforting smell, but not the Sustaining Sort of smell that would cheer a Bear in Need of Lunch. But don't worry. I believe we have come in the right direction, because my nose is listening very strongly to a very honeyish smell right now. Come on."

Scratch and sniff the lovely-
to-smell honeysuckle bush.
Will the smell cheer a
Hungry Pooh Bear?

Off they went, and for a long time Piglet said nothing, and then he made a squeaky noise, and then an oo-noise, because he had begun to know where they were, but still he didn't like to say anything in case they weren't. And just when he was getting so sure of himself that it didn't matter anymore, "There you are!" cried a familiar voice, and a Tigger who was not at all lost in the Hundred Acre Wood bounced out of the mist and knocked them flat.

After Pooh and Piglet explained that Rabbit was a very lost Rabbit at the Top of the Wood, and Tigger went off to find him, Pooh went home to have a Little Something, and Piglet went along to watch.

Scratch and sniff. *Finally*, Pooh's having his smackerel of delicious honey. Would you like a smackerel, too?

And while Pooh was having his honey, Tigger was bouncing around the Top of the Wood looking for Rabbit. And at last a very small and very sorry, an Oh-Tigger-I-am-glad-to-see-you-Rabbit heard old Tigger crashing about, and came running through the mist to be rescued. And it seemed to Rabbit that he had never seen such a Grand Tigger, such a Friendly Tigger, such a Tigger who bounced in just the big and beautiful way that a Tigger should bounce.

And Christopher Robin, when he heard the whole story, gave a party to celebrate the Grand and Wonderful Thing Tigger had done by Finding Rabbit, and Pooh made up a hum about the Wonderful Bounciness of Tiggers, and they all had gingerbread, and Roo had too much and had to go home early, and Pooh had honey on his, and Rabbit and Tigger sat together and chatted away like the best of friends.

Rabbit was very curious to know how Tigger had found his way back from the top of the Wood.

"Well, that's the Second Thing about Tiggers," said Tigger.

"Second Thing?" said Rabbit. "What's the First?"

"The First Thing about Tiggers," said Tigger, "is that they never stop bouncing. And the Second Thing is that they never get lost."

Here's a piece of the party
gingerbread for you to scratch
and sniff. Which do you like best,
gingerbread or honey? Which one
do you think Pooh likes best?